CLEAN GREEN MACHINES

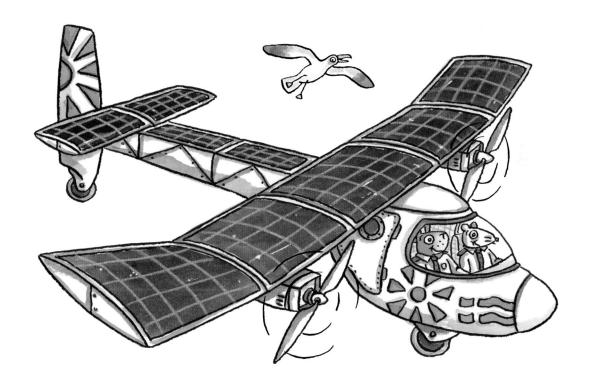

For Rufus, in hope of a cleaner, greener world—TM

KINGFISHER
LONDON & NEW YORK

Text copyright © Tony Mitton 2022
Illustrations copyright © Ant Parker 20221
Designed by Anthony Hannant (LittleRedAnt)

Published in the United States by Kingfisher,
120 Broadway, New York, NY 10271
Kingfisher is an imprint of Macmillan Children's Books, London.
All rights reserved
Distributed in the U.S. and Canada by Macmillan, 120 Broadway, New York, NY 10271

LIBRARY OF CONGRESS CATALOGING-IN-PUBLICATION DATA HAS BEEN APPLIED FOR

ISBN 978-0-7534-7680-2

Kingfisher books are available for special promotions and premiums. For details contact:
Special Markets Department, Macmillan, 120 Broadway, New York, NY 10271

For more information, please visit
www.kingfisherbooks.com

Printed in China
9 8 7 6 5 4 3 2 1

MIX
Paper from
responsible sources
FSC
www.fsc.org   FSC® C116313

whirr

CLEAN GREEN
MACHINES

Tony Mitton
and Ant Parker

KINGFISHER
LONDON & NEW YORK

These are solar panels.
They gather rays of sun,

then turn them into heat and light
and power for everyone.

Turbines have propeller blades,
and wind will make them turn.

They generate electric power
that many things can burn.

Water has tremendous force—
this dam's a smart machine.

It feeds a great big city
with energy that's clean.

Look at this: a green machine
that most of us will like—
a power-assisted vehicle,
a neat electric bike!

When you turn the pedals,
a dynamo inside
will generate electric power
to give a smoother ride.

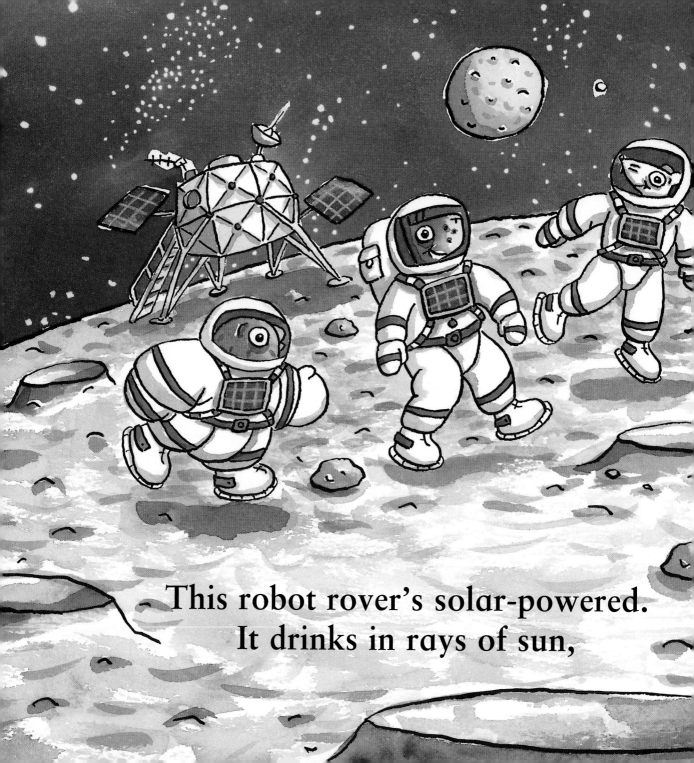

This robot rover's solar-powered.
It drinks in rays of sun,

which give it fuel to move around
and get its task-list done.

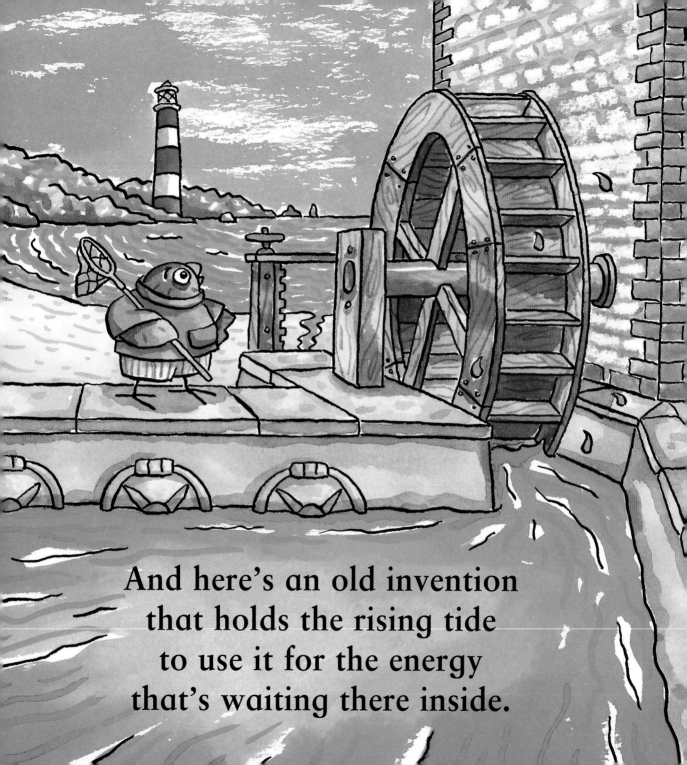

And here's an old invention
that holds the rising tide
to use it for the energy
that's waiting there inside.

When the tide goes out again
the water in the pool
runs out to power a flour mill—
how clever and how cool!

A solar plane can use the sun
to power it for its flight,

but cannot travel fast or far—
and not at all at night!

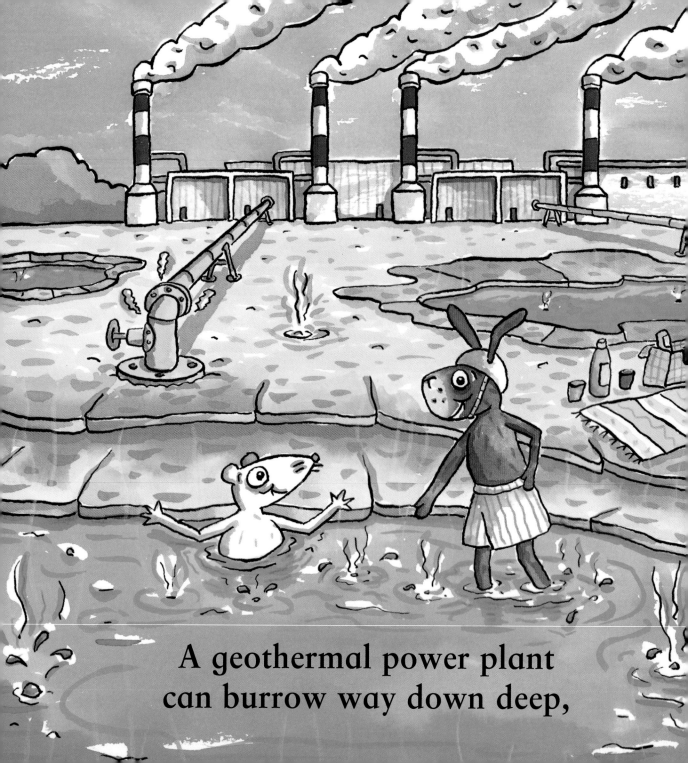

A geothermal power plant
can burrow way down deep,

for far beneath us, underground,
there's energy to reap.

A green machine we're working on,
but haven't made so far,

is this amazing vehicle:
the solar-powered car!

Machines use lots of energy
to do the things they do.

But some machines save energy,
and help to make it too.

Water power bits

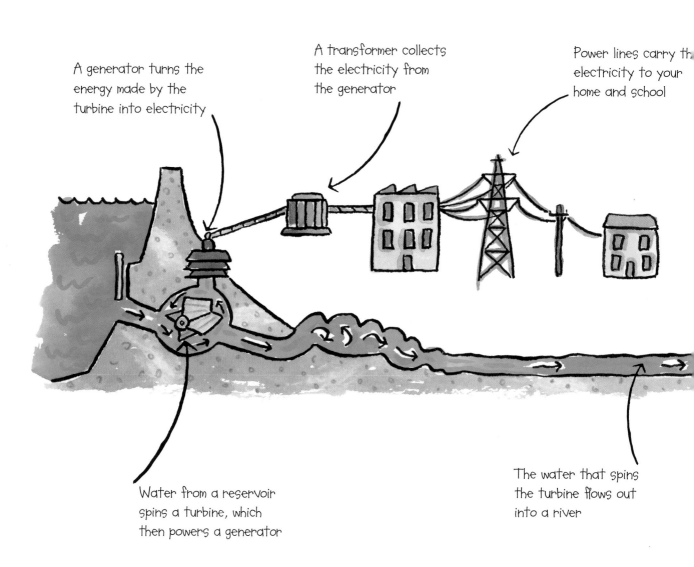

A generator turns the energy made by the turbine into electricity

A transformer collects the electricity from the generator

Power lines carry the electricity to your home and school

Water from a reservoir spins a turbine, which then powers a generator

The water that spins the turbine flows out into a river

Look out for these **AMAZING** books by Tony Mitton and Ant Parker!

Collect all the **AMAZING MACHINES** picture story books:

Or store them all in the **BIG TRUCKLOAD OF FUN**— the perfect gift for little ones:

Contains 14 Amazing Machines picture story books

Meet your favorite animals with the **AMAZING ANIMALS** series: